First

published

2017 by Walker

Books Ltd, 87 Vauxhall

Walk, London SE11 5HJ

Text © 2017 Mac Barnett

Illustrations © 2017 Jon Klassen

The moral rights of the author

and illustrator have been asserted

This book has been typeset in ITC New

Clarendon • Printed in China • All rights reserved.

 British Library Cataloguing in Publication

Data: a catalogue record for this book is available from the British

Library • ISBN 978-1-4063-7667-8 • www.walker.co.uk • 10 9 8 7 6 5 4 3 2 1

TRIANGLE

by

Mac Barnett

&

Jon Klassen

WALKER BOOKS
AND SUBSIDIARIES
LONDON · BOSTON · SYDNEY · AUCKLAND

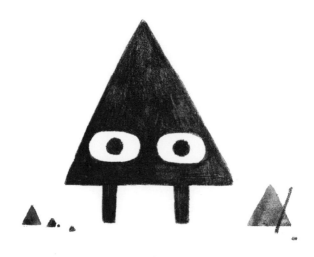

This is Triangle.

This is Triangle's house.

This is Triangle in his house.

And that is Triangle's door.

One day Triangle walked out of his door
and away from his house.

He was going to play a sneaky trick on Square.

He walked past small triangles

and medium triangles and big triangles.

He walked past shapes

that weren't triangles any more.

They were shapes

with no names.

He walked until he got to a place

where there were squares.

Still thinking of his sneaky trick,
he walked past big squares

and medium squares and small squares

until he got to Square's house.
"Now," said Triangle,

"I will play my sneaky trick."

Triangle walked up to Square's door

and said "HISS!" just like a snake.

Square was afraid of snakes.

"Oh me oh my!" said Square.

"Go away, you snake! Leave my door!"

"HISS!" said Triangle. "HISS! HISS! HISS!"

"Oh dear dear dear!" said Square.

"How many snakes are out there? Ten?
Ten million? Go away, snakes!"

Triangle could not hiss any more.
He was laughing too hard.

"Triangle!" said Square. "Is that you?"

"Yes!" said Triangle. "I know you are afraid of snakes. I have played a sneaky trick on you!"

Square ran after Triangle, past small squares

and medium squares and big squares.

He ran past the shapes

with no names,

past the big triangles

and medium triangles and small triangles,

up to Triangle's house and right through his door.

Almost.

"You are stuck!" Triangle laughed and laughed.

Then he stopped. His house was all dark.
Triangle was afraid of the dark.
"It's too dark!" said Triangle. "You're blocking
my light! Go away, you block! Leave my door!"

It was Square's turn to laugh.
"I know you are afraid of the dark. Now I have
played a sneaky trick on you! You see, Triangle,
this was my plan all along."

But do you really believe him?

To the Rexes: Adam, Marie, and Henry

M. B.

For Steve Malk

J. K.

MAC BARNETT & JON KLASSEN have made three books together: *Sam and Dave Dig a Hole,* which won a Caldecott Honor and an E. B. White Read Aloud Award; *Extra Yarn,* which won a Caldecott Honor, an E. B. White Read Aloud Award and a Boston Globe-Horn Book Award; and *Triangle,* which is the book you are reading right now. They both live in California, USA, but in different cities.